essential careers™

A **CAREER** AS A
# MOBILE APP DEVELOPER

JASON PORTERFIELD

**Rosen**
**YA**
New York

Published in 2018 by The Rosen Publishing Group, Inc.
29 East 21st Street, New York, NY 10010

Copyright © 2018 by The Rosen Publishing Group, Inc.

First Edition

**Library of Congress Cataloging-in-Publication Data**

Names: Porterfield, Jason, author.
Title: A career as a mobile app developer / Jason Porterfield.
Description: New York: Rosen Publishing, 2018. | Series: Essential careers | Includes bibliographical references and index. | Audience: Grades 7–12.
Identifiers: LCCN 2017015805 | ISBN 9781538381564 (library bound) | ISBN 9781508178729 (paperback)
Subjects: LCSH: Mobile apps—Vocational guidance—Juvenile literature. | Application software—Vocational guidance—Juvenile literature. | Computer software—Development—Vocational guidance—Juvenile literature.
Classification: LCC QA76.76.A65 P664 2018 | DDC 005.35—dc23
LC record available at https://lccn.loc.gov/2017015805

*Manufactured in China*

# contents

# INTRO

## Design

Mobile apps enable people to use their tablets and smartphones to perform many of the same functions as desktop or laptop computers.

# DUCTION

Evolving technology has made the world a much more connected place than it was just a few decades ago. People no longer have to find a landline telephone or log on to a computer to make a call or look at information online. Instead, they can pull powerful mobile devices out of their pockets and call someone or look up the information they need. Smartphones—and their larger counterparts, tablets—provide an enormous amount of computing power that people can use in any location where there's a wireless internet connection.

Mobile devices, primarily smartphones and tablets, can connect to the internet through programs called apps. These apps enable the mobile device's user to surf the internet, take pictures, make recordings, and perform numerous other tasks. Some mobile apps are extremely practical, such as those that provide maps. Other mobile apps such as games are just for fun. Mobile apps have played a big role in the growing popularity of smartphones. With these apps, the devices became tools that people could use to do everything from send messages to order food for delivery. Millions of mobile apps exist, and the demand for them continues to grow.

Mobile app developers are the people who create mobile apps. They take an idea, create a design, and write the code that brings the mobile app concept to life. Once the app has been tested, it's ready for release to the public. Generally, the mobile app is created for use on one kind of mobile device or through the World Wide Web, which is the part of the much larger internet that most people can access. The internet itself is a vast network of interconnected computers, databases, machine processors, handheld devices, and even appliances. Versions for other types of devices might be developed if the mobile app is popular enough. The process can take weeks or even months, depending on the complexity of the app.

Mobile app developers are in constant demand by large and small companies. Building a career as a mobile app developer requires a deep interest in programming, design skills, and an extensive knowledge of coding. Many mobile app developers become interested in coding when they are in high school or earlier. Some pursue this interest in school, while others learn their programming skills on their own. Some mobile app developers specialize in building apps for just one platform. Others have the knowledge to switch back and forth between platforms.

A college degree in computer science is generally seen as a requirement for entering the field. People who are interested in becoming mobile app developers can start by learning the basics of coding in high school classes, community college programs, or even by teaching themselves. By the time they earn their college degree, they'll be ready to step into the constantly growing and changing field of mobile app development.

# chapter 1

# THE MOBILE APP UNIVERSE

Since people began using the World Wide Web in the early 1990s, they have become more and more connected through their computers. In the decades since, the web has advanced from connections that relied on dial-up modems over telephone lines to wireless and fiber networks that can provide fast connections virtually anywhere.

The development of smartphones and tablets in the last decade has further increased the reach of the web. Connections are available in places where getting on the internet would once have been unimaginable.

## MOBILE CONNECTIONS

Mobile app development is the branch of information technology that exists around the design, development, and release of mobile apps. Mobile apps are created for smartphones and for tablets. The majority of mobile apps are built for devices that use either Apple's iOS operating system or Google's Android system. Other platforms do exist, however. Windows Phone is the most prominent of the less popular mobile platforms.

There are three types of mobile apps: native apps, web apps, and hybrid apps. Native apps are mobile apps that are built for one specific platform, or type of mobile device. These may be apps that work only on iPhones, Android smartphones, or

Yelp

Yelp, Inc

T Teen

*Hybrid apps such as Yelp are often simplified versions of websites that are designed to work across platforms for greater flexibility and ease of use.*

Similar

other specific mobile devices. Smartphone or tablet users install them directly from an online store, such as the Apple App Store, and use them by tapping an icon on their screen.

Web apps are mobile apps that are not installed directly on a device but instead load through a web browser such as Safari or Chrome. Users don't need to take up valuable storage space by storing these apps. They offer flexibility in terms of design and generally make it easier for consumers to use websites on their devices, but they nearly always require an internet connection to work.

Hybrid apps are a cross between native apps and web apps. They tend to be easier and less expensive to develop than native apps but are more powerful than standard web apps. Hybrid apps are built using the same languages as web apps, but they also include some native code that allows them to access some of the functionality of the mobile devices themselves.

App development is similar to creating other types of software in some ways. It requires a deep knowledge of computer language, precise coding skills, and great attention to detail. Creating mobile apps is also very different. Smartphones, tablets, and other mobile devices are much smaller than computers. The space and memory that can be dedicated to storing and using mobile apps is much smaller than that on laptops or desktop computers. Mobile app developers therefore must be able to work within a confined digital space to create the software that enables people to get the most out of their smartphones or tablets.

## ONLINE MENTALITY

Computer technology has advanced in ways that would have been unimaginable when the first computers were built during the 1940s and 1950s. Those machines were so large that they took up entire rooms—or even whole floors—of buildings.

Pioneering hardware developer Gordon Moore holds up a wafer of silicon, the material used to make the powerful microchips that led him to write Moore's Law.

They were so complex that it took teams of people just to get them to carry out a single function. Despite their massive size, they lacked the processing power of even the earliest desktop computers, which were first developed in the late 1970s and early 1980s. Even the earliest smartphones had more processing power than these supercomputers.

This shrinking came about because of the development of the microchip in 1959. It was no longer necessary to fill rooms with equipment to build a computer. As chip technology advanced, the computers that used them became more powerful and smaller in size. The principle behind the increase in processing power and the dramatic decrease in size—from gigantic machines that filled rooms to powerful devices that are smaller than a paperback book—is sometimes referred to as Moore's Law. It is named after Gordon Moore, who founded the Intel computer company. Moore's Law states that the number of computer processors that fit onto a given chip can be doubled every two years. That observation held true through the first decade of the twenty-first century, enabling faster, smaller, and more powerful computers to be built.

The invention of the World Wide Web in 1989 and its development gave people new ways to use their computers. In the past, computers were largely seen as business machines. Relatively few people had personal computers, and those who used computers almost always used them for work or school. The web made it possible to share data with people from all walks of life and from all around the world. Improvements in transmission technology and falling computer prices helped put the web in millions of homes and make it the vital part of modern life that it is today. Many people now rely on the web to communicate, pay their bills, deliver important documents, shop, and perform numerous ot her tasks that are vital to daily life.

## THE CONNECTED WORLD

The invention of smartphones during the first decade of the twenty-first century sparked a revolution in the way in which people communicate and use the web. The development of affordable laptops during the 1990s had already freed people from having to use the internet from a desk, but smartphones allowed much more freedom. Finally, people could perform tasks online by using a device that is small enough to carry around in a pocket.

As revolutionary as the development of the smartphone has been, smartphones were not the first mobile devices to use apps. Some early cell phones had relatively simple apps, such as calendars and calculators, that performed practical functions, as well as simple games. Personal digital assistants (PDAs) were first developed in the mid-1990s. These devices were about the same size as a smartphone and helped people keep track of appointments and contact information and manage other useful details.

During the 1990s, a software company, Psion, developed an operating system for PDAs called EPOC. EPOC enabled people with PDAs that were technologically advanced enough to use word-processing programs, databases, diary programs, and spreadsheets. Later versions of EPOC allowed users to add additional programs through software packages. The Palm operating system followed on EPOC's heels. Developed in 1996, Palm's PDAs came with numerous basic apps and the option to add more apps from third-party developers.

Apps really first took off in popularity with the development of the Symbian operating system in 2001. Symbian was developed as a joint project between several mobile phone companies—Nokia, Ericsson, Psion, and Motorola. It was based on later versions of EPOC and widely marketed on Nokia phones. In 2009, Symbian was on 250 million mobile phones, mostly those manufactured by Nokia, as well as some devices from Samsung and LG. Symbian looked much like modern smartphone operating systems look, with colorful icons indicating useful apps such as a browser and a calculator.

BlackBerry OS was developed for BlackBerry Limited's (later Research in Motion, or RIM) line of smartphones. The operating system was released in 2002 and included a wide variety of mobile apps that were useful for businesspeople. BlackBerry OS's email, calendars, address books, and planner functions helped make BlackBerry's mobile devices very popular until Apple's iPhone and smartphones using Google's Android operating system took much of the company's business away.

Apple's iOS platform was developed in 2007 to work exclusively on the company's mobile devices, including the iPhone, the iPod Touch music player, and the iPad tablet. The user interface is based on a touchscreen system and includes a variety of digital buttons, graphic icons, and "sliders" that allow the user to swipe left, right, up, or down within the operating system or the apps themselves.

Early smartphones from Nokia and other manufacturers ran on the Symbian platform. The platform displayed apps as colorful touch-screen icons that would look familiar to iPhone and Android users.

Android, which was also developed in 2007, is Google's answer to iOS. It works in much the same way through touchscreen functions and controls. However, it was designed to be used on smartphones, tablets, and mobile devices marketed by many different technology companies.

Since their rollout, iOS and Android have been the two most widely used operating systems on the market. Mobile app developers tend to choose to create apps for one or the other, or sometimes for both.

## A THRIVING MARKET

Smartphone usage continues to grow as the devices become easier for people to afford. A survey conducted by the Pew Research Center in early 2017 found that 77 percent of Americans owned a smartphone of some type. In 2011, that number was 35 percent. Among people ages eighteen

# THE iPHONE REVOLUTION

The release of the first version of Apple's iPhone in 2007 marked the beginning of a major shift in how people communicate and access the internet. There had been smartphones previously, namely BlackBerry and Nokia mobile devices. Although those companies made popular products, the iPhone managed to appeal to a broad audience with extra features, including a built-in music player, a camera, and touchscreen controls. Even more functions could be accessed when users downloaded mobile apps onto their iPhones.

The iPhone became enormously popular, sparking the growth of the smartphone revolution. Google and Windows developed their own products as a response to the iPhone. Although the iPhone may not have been the first smartphone, it was the device that introduced many people to mobile computing.

to twenty-nine, a staggering 92 percent owned a smartphone, while 88 percent of those ages thirty-three to forty-nine had one. Roughly 51 percent of Americans owned a tablet, and 22 percent said that they have an electronic reader that they use to read ebooks. Approximately 12 percent of adults in the United States access the internet exclusively through their smartphones and do not have traditional broadband service at home.

With such a strong market in place, an intense demand for apps exists even though there are millions of apps already in existence. In 2015, Windows announced that it had more than 669,000 apps in its app store, though that total includes apps designed for desktop computers.

Google offers more than 2.2 million mobile apps for Android devices through its online store, Google Play. Apple has more than two million apps available at its App Store, which launched in 2008. Those apps have been in demand, with Apple reporting that apps from

*Mobile apps make it easy to do homework in any setting. Students can use their smartphones for tasks such as setting up study schedules, finding information, and watching video tutorials.*

the App Store have been downloaded 130 billion times since it opened. Apple App Store customers have spent more than $50 million on apps in that time.

There are apps for nearly anything that a person can imagine. Some apps come from a very real demand, while others are clever ideas that the developers hope will catch on and become popular. They may be tools for watching movies on a smartphone, or filters for photos, or a way to shop online. Some apps are for on-demand services, meaning that a customer uses them and the service they seek becomes available almost immediately. Ride-sharing services such as Uber and Lyft rely on on-demand apps. Other apps might schedule a time in the future when a client can receive a service, even if that time is just a short while from when the client used the app. These apps can be used to schedule everything from salon appointments to food deliveries. The games that people play on smartphones are apps, as are the programs that help them keep track of what they have eaten during the day.

App usage is widespread. About 85 percent of the time that people spend on smartphones is devoted to using apps, according to a 2015 study conducted by Forrester Research. While they spend a lot of time with their apps and there are millions of apps to choose from, most people also have an upper limit to the number of apps they can use. Typically, most people use just five apps most of the time. It's not the same five for everyone. In a given month, people may use just twenty-six or twenty-seven apps, regardless of how many they have on their mobile devices.

The apps that are most commonly used are social media and communication apps, according to Forrester Research. About 21 percent of smartphone minutes are spent on these apps, which include everything from Twitter to Facebook. Other leading categories of apps include games, news, streaming video, books and magazines, shopping, maps, and productivity apps associated with careers.

With so many apps available and just a few types of apps competing for the majority of smartphone users' attention, app designers have to be sure that their apps will be interesting enough and useful enough to get attention. Businesses can do this by targeting their best and most loyal customers with apps that will make it easier for them to make more transactions, for example. Companies and organizations sometimes offer apps that people can download for free to draw attention to a particular product or cause. There is still plenty of room for talented and creative app developers to make a mark with a hot new game or service app.

# chapter 2

## GETTING STARTED WITH APPS

Mobile app development is a career that requires many different talents, as well as a passion for creating new and useful software. More than anything, mobile app developers need to know how to write the codes that give apps the instructions they need to function properly. This expertise requires a deep knowledge of programming for their chosen platform.

Knowing how to create computer programs is not sufficient, however. Mobile app developers should also understand how to design an app that will work well within the limitations of mobile technology. To be successful, they should also have a solid understanding of the types of mobile apps that people want.

### KNOWING PROGRAMMING

At its most basic level, app development is computer programming for smaller devices. There are also some major differences. The size constraints can be significant for programmers who are used to having access to more memory and drive space. They also have to work with screens that are several times smaller than desktop or laptop computers. Programmers may also be used to working in an atmosphere where adding more features is going to improve the application. With mobile apps, that isn't always the case.

Apps are developed in two ways. In the first, the app is written with a web browser in mind as its main means of delivery. In many ways, this is the simpler method. The app only has to be written once, and different versions can be set up for different platforms. A single programming language can be used, and shortcuts can be taken with pieces of code that already exist.

The second mobile app development method requires writing a separate app for each platform. This method is more expensive and takes longer, but it also has several advantages. A dedicated mobile app built specifically for a particular device will perform better than one built to be used across platforms. It can also perform a wider range of functions than a web-based app. It can store data, interact with other apps on the mobile device, and make use of the mobile device's controls—all of which are functions that are impossible with a web-based app.

Certain programming languages are better for some types of mobile apps than others. Learning as many programming languages as possible gives mobile app developers the flexibility to build a wide variety of apps. The most common languages associated with mobile app development are Python, Swift, Java, Ruby on Rails, C++, and HTML 5.

HTML 5 is an all-purpose programming language that is used for web development. It can be used to build web-based mobile apps and is gradually becoming the standard web programming language. HTML 5 makes it easy to add data types and adapt apps to different screen sizes, and it works across many different browsers. Another language, Javascript, can be useful for adding extra features to web-based mobile apps.

Java can be used for both browser-based programming or for creating separate apps. This flexibility makes it easy to update software and reuse code for other apps. Developers who focus on mobile apps for devices that use the Android platform will need to know Java. The language is also useful for building a code base that can work across several different platforms.

```
string4replace = string4r
): value = float(value) te
format = 14 #Replace string
(key)) tempString = tempString.
value*pow(10,14-tmpFormat)))))
(typeOfFID == "BUFFER"): s =
+ tempString.replace("czFieldID",
(typeOfFID == "ASCII_STRING")
) tempString = tempString.
<name value=" in line ar
</Message>" in line:
lyFilename+"\n" if type
os.path.exists(path):
shut
```

Professional mobile app *developers* often have years of experience in coding in at least one programming *language*, whether they learned it in school or on their own.

C++ is useful for programming mobile apps for Windows and Android platforms. The language has been around since the early 1980s and has long been a popular choice among programmers. It is powerful and flexible, making it ideal for creating mobile apps that can interact with other applications.

Swift is a relatively new language that was created by Apple for building mobile apps that utilize the iOS platform. It's an all-purpose programming language and has been designed to eliminate the security flaws that sometimes arose with older programming languages.

Two of the most popular languages for developing web apps for mobile devices are Python and Ruby on Rails. Python is a flexible and simple language that can be used for creating web apps and hybrid apps, particularly games. Ruby on Rails can be used to quickly build mobile web apps that work well across multiple platforms. It is frequently used to develop business-related apps and has been adapted by many start-ups, as well as by long-established companies and organizations such as Amazon and the National Aeronautics and Space Administration (NASA).

Many mobile app developers use frameworks to create their apps. A mobile app framework functions as a software library that forms an underlying structure around which apps can be built for a specific platform. Several powerful frameworks exist for building hybrid mobile apps, including IONIC, Sencha Touch, and Kendo UI.

## DEVELOPMENT PLATFORM SPRINGBOARDS

Mobile apps are often built using platforms, which are programs that allow developers to quickly construct, test, and distribute their mobile apps. They are secure places where a developer can write code then use tools to test the mobile app to see whether it works properly. The development platform simulates how the mobile app will work on an actual device.

The Google Play Store is similar to the Apple App Store in many ways. Users can search for, purchase, and download a wide variety of apps for their Android devices.

Development platforms can be specific to the type of mobile app launched. Apple requires that all of the apps that are sold in the App Store be developed using the company's Integrated Development Environment, called Xcode. Mobile apps for Android can be built within Android Studios, and those for Windows Phone are built through the Universal Windows Platform.

There are numerous platform options for people who don't know any programming languages but want to experiment with mobile app construction and design. These platforms use visual editors that allow users to drag components into the app and drop them into place. Many allow users to create mobile apps that can use the mobile device's resources and connect with other apps.

The introduction of improved mobile devices and the opening of online stores for iOS, Android, and Windows Phone apps have contributed to a good ecosystem in which high-quality mobile apps can develop. With a powerful means of using them and a good environment for sharing them, mobile apps have taken off.

## UNDERSTANDING DESIGN

Considering that there are millions of mobile apps available, mobile app developers pay particular attention to design when creating an app. It has to be powerful enough to serve its purpose, easy to use, and small enough to function on a mobile device. Customers should want to use it instead of similar apps.

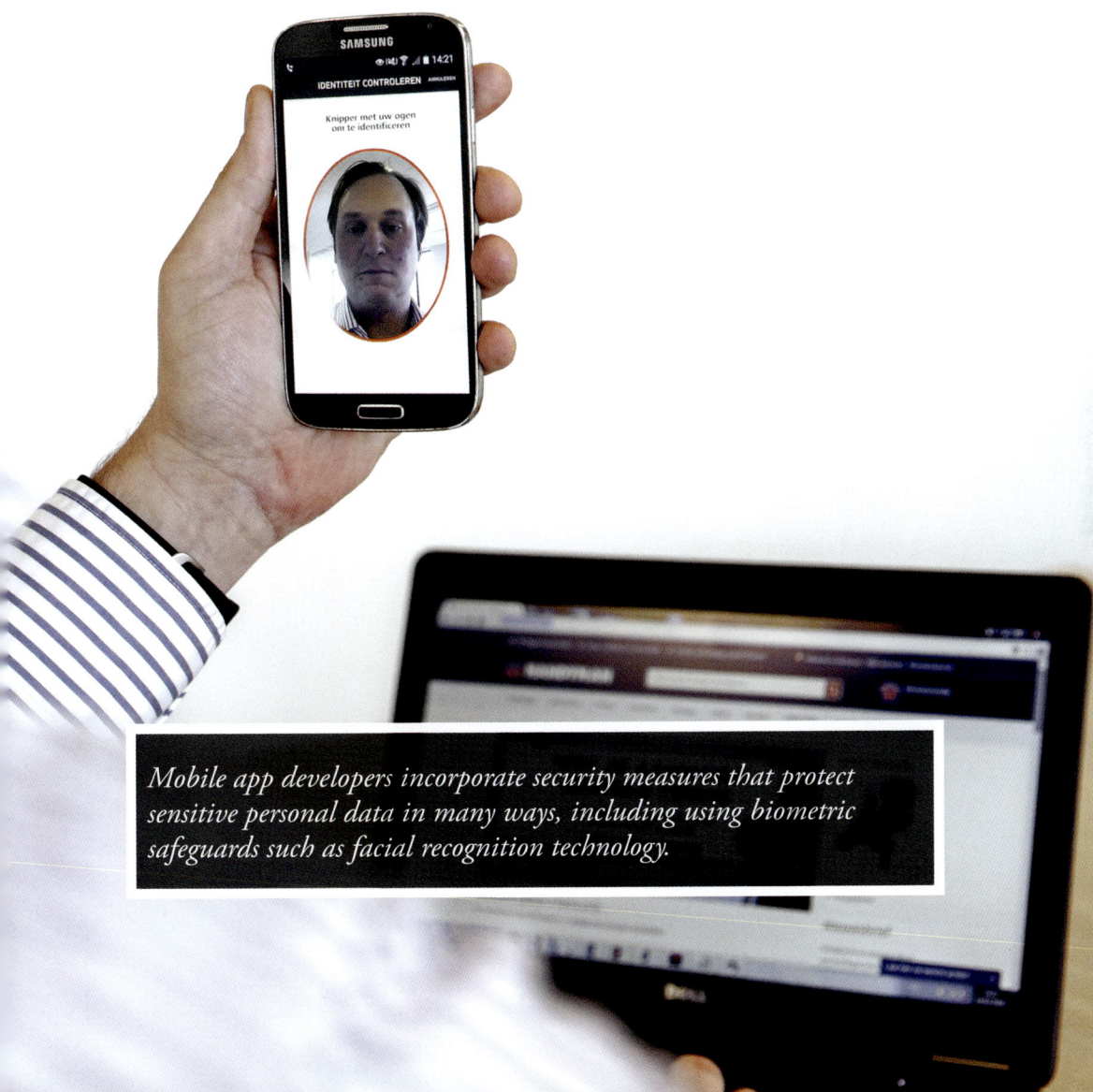

*Mobile app developers incorporate security measures that protect sensitive personal data in many ways, including using biometric safeguards such as facial recognition technology.*

Anyone who is thinking about becoming a mobile app designer should start looking at the apps that are already available. Many mobile app developers compare apps to figure out what design elements they like. If they're interested in web apps for mobile devices or mobile-ready websites, they might look at how these apps differ from platform to platform. The design scheme for Facebook's mobile app looks quite different depending on whether one uses the version for iOS, Android, or Windows Phone, for example.

The three major platforms have style and functionality guidelines for mobile app developers. The guidelines are available to the public and can be found online. They can give mobile app developers an idea of how apps should look and how they should work for mobile device users.

## HACKED APPS

Mobile devices are designed to be highly secure, but mobile apps themselves can become points of vulnerability. Some mobile apps are created to mimic legitimate apps with the intention of stealing important personal data. Researchers from the cybersecurity company Check Point discovered in 2016 that hackers had used fake mobile apps to create access points to more than 1.3 million Google accounts. The accounts had not yet been compromised, but email addresses, photo collections, and other personal files were vulnerable. The malicious mobile apps also installed advertising software that was designed to track the accounts of mobile device users.

Apple's mobile devices using the iOS platform are also vulnerable to hackers. In 2015, mobile apps that were developed using a counterfeit version of Apple's Xcode development software were found in the App Store. The infected mobile apps carry malware called XcodeGhost that can collect and steal data such as login information.

Mobile apps should also be created to be secure against hackers and data thieves. Mobile devices themselves are designed with multiple levels of security protections in place. However, third-party apps are sometimes vulnerable to hackers. Security is a growing concern with mobile apps, as more people use their smartphones and tablets to access sensitive information. Mobile app developers need to know how to design their apps so that they don't have any vulnerabilities that are easy to exploit. This situation requires creating solid authentication and authorization processes, developing strong cryptography, and making sure the app isn't leaking personal information.

Many software companies—and companies that create mobile apps—have processes in place for creating their programs. The software development cycle is a series of steps that carries the basic idea for an app to its completion. By following these steps, mobile app developers can ensure that they are building high-quality software. In its simplest form, the software development cycle consists of analyzing the needs of users, designing the program, writing the code, analyzing and testing the program, and then supporting and updating it so that it will remain useful and usable. Understanding this process and following it helps mobile app developers create software that people will want to use and that works seamlessly.

## WHAT USERS WANT

Understanding the market for mobile apps is key to successfully launching an app. With so many products out there and so much competition, mobile app developers need to have a good idea of what people want from their apps.

One of the biggest factors contributing to a mobile app's appeal is the context in which it is used. Native mobile apps exist to be used exclusively for their intended purpose. You probably won't have any reason to use a restaurant's mobile app unless you plan to visit that restaurant. Because there are so many apps competing for users' attention, it is extremely important to find a way to help users get the information they want as quickly as possible. Web apps are more flexible, even though they may not be as powerful or work as well as a native mobile app.

Native mobile app developers are somewhat limited by the technology. Even the most powerful mobile devices do not have the memory space, storage space, or bandwidth that larger computers possess. Apps for mobile devices have to be designed with these limitations in mind. The graphics have to be small enough and clear enough that they can fit on a smartphone screen and still be functional, and the controls must be easy to use and understand.

Web apps for mobile devices also face limitations. Mobile apps lack the "hover" state that laptops and desktops share, in which a mouse or trackpad can be used to move the cursor so that it hovers over links and other features. It is also more

Smartphones and other mobile devices are convenient for looking up information. However, the small screen size can limit one's ability to spend a lot of time reading and taking notes.

difficult to type on a smartphone or tablet, and the screen size limits the amount of information that can be displayed at one time. This smaller size can make it hard to tap on the right part of the screen to activate a feature or access a link. Memory limitations can slow web apps for mobile devices to a crawl.

Mobile app developers test the features of their apps for limitations and problems in their mobile development platforms. These platforms give them a digital environment in which they can run the application and simulate how it will look on an actual smartphone or tablet. They use these environments to make sure the app can work as intended. Adjustments can be made as they work until the app is streamlined, easy to use, and performing as expected.

Creating a successful mobile app can be as simple as finding a shortcoming in an existing app. Developers might notice that shopping apps don't perform a particular function that would make them easier to use on mobile devices, for example. They may create a similar app that fills in the missing service while performing many of the same tasks as other apps. This simple improvement can make a tremendous difference. User feedback also drives app development and improvements. Users may request customization options or the ability to use an app across platforms, leading to new versions of the mobile app.

# chapter 3

# AN APP EDUCATION

M obile app development is a career choice that anyone with strong math skills, creativity, and the ability to learn coding can follow. Many successful apps have been developed by high school and even middle school students. Others are built by independent contractors or by self-taught hobbyists. Once the app is developed and distributed, the developer's background does not matter much. However, anyone who wants to become a professional mobile app developer for an information technology (IT) company needs to have a degree in a computer science-related field before that person can be hired.

Getting an early start can prolong one's career and lead to more opportunities. Some mobile app developers become interested in programming at a very early age. They may work with basic programming tools in elementary school or start learning to code. Others may not become interested until middle school or high school, when more computer science classes are available.

## BUILDING A FOUNDATION

The foundations for a career in mobile app development are typically established in high school. Math and science classes are particularly important. Mobile app developers often need

Students who take programming classes in high school will be able to get help from enthusiastic teachers and fellow students who share their interest in computers.

to use mathematics when writing code. The ability and the patience to work complex equations is necessary in environments where coding is involved. Many college-level computer science programs require students to take classes in calculus, physics, statistics, engineering, and other sciences that utilize analytical skills. Laboratory sciences such as chemistry and biology teach experimental processes, even if these subjects don't seem to have anything to do with computer science.

Many high school computer science programs offer classes that teach students programming in several languages. Every language mastered in high school is a language that an app developer doesn't have to learn in college. Some high schools offer specialized computer science classes. Students should take any classes that cover mobile app development. Courses on game development or digital animation can be helpful to anyone who wants to build games for mobile devices, for instance.

# APP DEVELOPMENT BOOT CAMPS

Students can prepare themselves for classes in software development by entering intense programs called boot camps. These classes are operated by private companies and generally last for several months. Participants pay fees to study mobile app development for iOS, Android, and Windows devices. Some app development boot camps are held online through video lectures, while others are built around in-person classes.

Depending on the program, students might learn the basics of working in several coding languages, complete an app on their own, or participate in a group project that mimics what it's like to work on a mobile app development team. Boot camps can be a good way to gain the coding knowledge you'll need in your college-level classes, but they often require a great deal of focus and self-discipline. If you sign up for a boot camp, you have to commit to doing the assignments to make the course worth your time.

Future mobile app developers should explore other electives that they are passionate about. Those interests can lead to breakthroughs in app development. An interest in photography or film could inspire a student to create new mobile apps for editing images, or a drama student might develop an app for helping actors memorize their lines.

Engineering and art classes are useful to mobile app developers. Both teach students about design. Engineering courses can help students create mobile apps that are efficient and logical through a series of steps that are like those used in app development. Art classes can teach students how to design apps that are attractive and that people will want to use. Future mobile app developers might look at after-school activities that can help them learn about the field. Clubs and meet-up groups are good ways to get to know other people who are interested in mobile app development.

Many school districts offer vocational school programs to high school students and graduates that can teach them how to code. It can take several months or even a year or two to complete these courses, but graduates can earn a certificate showing that they are proficient in coding. Vocational certificates can be very useful when looking for an entry-level IT job and also look good on college applications.

## LEARNING AND INTERNING

Internships offer a great way for people who want to be mobile app developers to gain some hands-on experience in the field. Interns work for a company for a specified period of time and usually for little or no pay, though some offer a small stipend to cover living expenses. The student's school may also offer academic credit for completing an internship. The intern benefits by learning about the company, how it works, and what the day-to-day job is like. The company benefits by having a bright and enthusiastic young person performing tasks that serve the business.

Typically, interns are asked to carry out some of the more low-level parts of projects, rather than tackling areas that might be vital to a projects' overall successes. These duties do not mean that they simply fetch coffee and scan documents. They may be asked to participate in planning sessions or even get to try their hand at coding.

*Middle school and high school students sometimes create mobile apps that make a huge difference, such as this medical app developed by seventh grader Tori Lawrence.*

Be careful of internship offers that make big promises but fail to deliver. Some companies take advantage of their interns by promising them work in one area, only to have them performing completely unrelated tasks. If you can, it's a good idea to talk to other students who have served in internships to find out what their experiences were like and what to expect.

Some of the larger technology companies seek out promising high school students. Facebook, for example, operates a summer internship called Facebook Academy geared toward local high school students. Start-ups also seek out promising students to serve as interns. Students might even get to design their own apps for marketing to the general public.

School guidance counselors might have tips for finding internships that are related to app development in your region. If there's nothing available, you might consider taking another IT-related internship. An internship in coding, network administration, or another IT field can help you gain valuable work experience and make contacts with people in your field. You might even be able to turn the internship into a job that lasts through your remaining high school years or into college. Your computer science teachers might also be able to give you information about large companies that offer internships or even smaller firms and start-ups that would be willing to bring a promising student on board for a short-term job. Websites for job seekers often list internships. Be sure to check whether they are open to high school students or to students who are already in college.

## SOFT SKILLS

Mobile app developers need skills other than the ability to code to ensure their success in the field. Many of these are skills that are picked up during high school. Time management is vital for building mobile apps, particularly

*Science-related activities, such as building robots for competitions, require many of the same problem-solving and organizational skills that mobile app builders need.*

if you've been hired to help meet a particular deadline. You have to be able to set aside enough time to come up with a design, write the code, conduct testing, and then make corrections. Computer science students will likely have practice at coming up with and completing big projects on time.

As your mobile app development career advances, you may take on more responsibilities. You may progress from working as one of several developers who share tasks to leading a development team. You'll have to know how to plan a project, delegate responsibilities, and keep everyone motivated to finish the job. You'll need to be able to devise and stick to a budget if you're working for a start-up with few cash resources. If you're leading the effort to develop a new mobile app, you might have to consider whether you need more employees to finish the job on time.

Becoming involved in various clubs and extracurricular activities at your school can prepare you for these responsibilities. Look for activities that interest you, whether they're related to programming or not. Becoming a club officer can help you learn how to handle responsibility. At the same time, you'll have the support of your faculty adviser and fellow officers to guide you.

Public speaking skills can prove useful to mobile app developers. Good oral and written communication skills are essential for getting your ideas across to members of your team and other stakeholders. You may be asked to write a report or give a presentation on a mobile app you've just developed or on a project you're working on. Even explaining elements of your mobile app's design to other members of your team can be a nerve-wracking experience for some people. Becoming involved in activities that encourage speaking in front of a crowd—such as school plays and a debate team— can help you become comfortable and confident when giving talks, regardless of the size of the audience.

Art skills are not a requirement for mobile app designers, but they are beneficial. Many mobile app developers create physical sketches of what their apps will look like on a screen. It's helpful to be able to accurately establish how proportions and perspectives will appear before you start coding. Some mobile game designers even study human anatomy and biology to get a feel for how bodies move. When it comes to creating the look of mobile games and other apps, many mobile app developers use graphic design software such as the Adobe Creative Suite. Classes on graphic design are available at many high schools.

## CERTIFICATIONS

Students can get an early start in mobile app development by earning a professional certification. Certifications are professional designations showing that a person has proven that she or he has demonstrated the ability to succeed within a given field. These certifications are generally available through commercial training courses from places such as the Mobile Development Institute and online learning programs such as Simplilearn. Community colleges also offer certificates in mobile app development. Certifications may take several weeks or even months to earn and may cover multiple classes, or they may simply focus on one area. Students will learn about programming within a mobile system, including the use of sensors, the user interface, working within hardware and memory limitations, and designing graphics. Certifications can help students land entry-level positions with software companies by showing that they have the skills necessary to complete many of the tasks that would be required of them. Certifications are available in mobile app development for iOS, Windows, and Android. Some programs offer certification in other areas related to mobile app development, such as mobile security analysis.

*Students in mobile app development programs learn how to take an idea from its earliest stages to the point where it becomes a useful app.*

## COLLEGE PROGRAMS

A bachelor's degree is commonly seen as a prerequisite for landing a job as a mobile app developer. Some students begin their college journey at a community college or a vocational school. There, they may earn credits that can be transferred to a four-year college. Earning a professional certificate or an associate's degree from one of these schools can help you get some basic required classes out of the way so that you can focus on more advanced-level computer science classes.

Many colleges and universities with strong IT departments offer majors in app development. The courses require a solid knowledge of programming languages and platforms. Prospective students should have coding experience before entering these programs.

The University of Southern California's Information Technology Program offers students an opportunity to focus on mobile app development for the most common mobile platforms, including Android, iOS, and Windows.

Stanford University offers a free online mobile app development class focusing on how to build mobile apps for iOS devices. It also encourages collaboration, offering a glimpse of what mobile app development would be like in the professional world. Carnegie-Mellon University offers a project-based online course that focuses on creating apps for the iPad. The university's on-campus mobile app offerings include a hands-on class that teaches students about topics such as how to deliver content in real time.

The University of California–Berkeley provides a full program on mobile app development for iOS and Android devices. The Massachusetts Institute of Technology (MIT) offers several courses on mobile app development through the school's computer science program, including courses on developing apps for iPhones. MIT's computer science program has also made a valuable tool called the App Inventor available to the general public. Designed for Android devices, the App Inventor enables people with even the most basic level of programming knowledge to develop their own apps.

College-level mobile app development classes often require students to take a project from the planning level to completion within a semester. Students may build mobile apps on their own or as part of a small team that mimics development teams at large companies. They'll come up with an idea for a mobile app and decide who their audience will be. They may get to choose the platform they'll program for, or they may be confined to working with a particular platform. They'll come up with a workable design, do the coding, and test it for flaws before presenting it. They may even have to come up with a plan for marketing the app. (Consider taking some marketing classes to develop marketing skills and business classes to help with converting the mobile app into a successful money-making venture.) The finished mobile app will likely be tested and graded based on factors such as usability, design, and whether it adequately performs its function. The developers may even have to give a formal presentation of their finished mobile app, just as they would in a workplace setting. By the time the class has finished, the students will have a thorough understanding of what it's like to create a mobile app.

# chapter 4

# THE MOBILE APP DEVELOPER JOB HUNT

S killed mobile app developers are in demand, as companies look to make an initial splash in the market or build on past successes. There are many jobs available from technology and communications companies that mainly deal in software and information technology. Some of these potential employers are industry giants. Others are scrappy start-ups that are hoping to gain a foothold in a competitive market. A mobile app developer shouldn't stop the job hunt there, however. Many businesses that may not appear to have anything to do with mobile devices on the surface are beginning to tap into the commercial potential of mobile apps.

## PREPARING FOR A JOB SEARCH

Earning a college degree puts mobile app developers in a good position to start a career, but the job search can take a while. Even though mobile app development is a growing field and more opportunities are always opening up, there are many talented people competing for those jobs. It's best to start getting ready for the job search before graduating. Job hunters who are still enrolled can draw on support from classmates, professors, and college resources.

Your college's career center is a good place to start looking for the perfect mobile app development job. Many colleges and university career centers provide workshops to help students with important job-seeking elements such as how to dress, interview skills, and assistance with cover letters and other communications. They can help students present themselves to interviewers as knowledgeable about their field of study. Career centers also coach students to show confidence and poise when answering questions during an interview and teaching them to make eye contact, speak clearly, and show good posture.

One of the most important aspects of the post-college job hunt is putting together a good résumé. A résumé is a brief document that describes a person's educational background, work experience, and any professional skills or areas of expertise that he or she may have acquired over time. Any student who has worked as an intern has probably created a résumé. Even some summer jobs require applicants to submit a résumé.

A recent college graduate's résumé shows where he or she went to high school and college. The applicant's major or concentration will be highlighted. If he or she participated in an honors program or studied abroad, that information should be listed. Club memberships, volunteer work, and extracurricular activities of all types help the applicant show a well-rounded personality. Summer jobs, internships, and any professional certifications should be included.

Recruiters look at the way the résumé is organized, whether it is formatted correctly, and whether everything is factually accurate. They'll check for spelling and serious grammatical errors. Even the way that the applicant describes his or her experience can mean the difference between getting hired and being rejected. Many recruiters like to see résumés that use an active voice, rather than simply listing accomplishments and work tasks. The career center can review résumés and offer pointers on how to make them stronger.

The career center can also help you assemble a portfolio, which is a collection of your best work. Your portfolio should include any mobile apps that you've developed. They can be

Career centers offer many services to job seekers, including presentations on how to choose a career path and tips on following through with those plans.

apps that you've built in your spare time, school projects that earned good grades, or apps that you've built during an internship. The portfolio gives potential employers a glimpse of the kind of work you can do. If you've developed apps for more than one mobile platform, try to include an example of each so that recruiters can see that you're able to work within different development platforms.

Online communities can be good places to learn about job openings. Many mobile app developers take part in message boards and other forums where they discuss their projects and offer one another tips and advice. Community members often come from many different backgrounds and experience levels, from professionals who have been developing mobile apps for years to amateur enthusiasts who are still in high school. Professionals may offer information about job openings. If you spend time hanging out in online communities, you'll probably learn about

# Résumé Tips from the Pros

Technology writer Priya Viswanathan has explored mobile technology since 2006. Writing for the tech website Lifewire (https://www.lifewire.com), she offers advice on building a résumé that shows off your mobile app development skills:

1.  Be sure to provide all details about your app developer skills, previous experience, posts previously held, and so on and also chalk out a list of recommendations you have received, as and when applicable.
2.  Though it is important that you list your academic qualifications, know that it is not going to take the first place in your bio-data, unless you are working in some kind of super specialized area. Mobile app development is something that is dynamic and always changing. Hence, your previous college certificate is not really going to hold water.
3.  Give all details about your past work history. List out your work history and give clear details of your past short-term developer jobs, explaining why they had been short-lived.

(Source: Viswanathan, Priya. "How to Write an Impressive Mobile App Developer Resume." October 19, 2016. https://www.lifewire.com/how-to-write-an-impressive-mobile-app-developer-resume-2373170.)

different developer tools and languages, as well as get an idea of what it is like to work in the field as a professional. You may even get to share some of your own expertise with other community members.

Online communities can also be a great place to learn about freelance opportunities. Freelance mobile app developers are hired for short-term projects on a temporary basis. They are given a contract to complete a particular job by a certain deadline and are paid when they meet this obligation. If their employer is satisfied with their work, it could lead to more freelance jobs, or the mobile app developer could even be hired on a full-time basis. Many mobile app developers who have not earned a college degree work as freelance developers. It's a good way to gain valuable professional experience, make important connections within the industry, and add more material to your portfolio.

Check online job boards for openings for mobile app developers as well. Some of the biggest job search sites—such as Monster, CareerBuilder, and Indeed—may have many listings for mobile app developers in your area. Check for opportunities from big IT companies and start-ups, but also keep an open mind about related work. You may find a job developing mobile apps for local governments, schools, retailers, restaurants, or even sports teams.

## SURVIVING A JOB INTERVIEW

Job interviews can be very stressful, but preparing for them helps reduce that stress. Be sure to dress appropriately. It's a good idea to dress formally to show that you take the process seriously. Have multiple copies of your résumé ready, as well as samples from your portfolio. The questions an interviewer asks are meant to gauge your level of interest in the job and whether you'd be a good fit. You might be asked why you want the job, what you can contribute to the team, and where you see yourself working in five years. The interviewer may ask you to go into detail about information on your résumé, such as a particular class you took or an internship you completed.

Making a good first impression is important during job interviews. Dressing nicely, making eye contact, and having a solid portfolio of work with you can help.

You should also have questions ready for the interviewer to show your own interest in the position. You might ask about the company's direction in the next few years, details about how development teams are structured, or the types of mobile apps you would be building.

After the interview, it's a good idea to send a brief message to thank the interviewer for the opportunity. You should avoid asking about the status of your application until a few days have passed, and only if you have not heard back. If all goes well, you may be contacted and either called in for a second interview or told that the job is yours.

## WORKING THE NETWORK

Mobile app developers may land their first jobs in several ways. They may send out dozens of résumés and cover letters to prospective employers, highlighting their qualifications and their experience. Others use their networking skills to

**Louiza Nolan**
597 Lancaster Drive
Bridgeport, CT 06606
Home: (203) 932-5849 Cell: (203) 895-3817 • lnolan34@gmail.com

## OBJECTIVE
A position as a mobile app developer that enables me to use my programming and design skills to create mobile apps for multiple platforms.

## EDUCATION
Central High School, 2009
B.S., Massachusetts Institute of Technology, 2013, Computer Science and Engineering

## WORK EXPERIENCE
2013–Present: **Mobile App Developer, Plover Software**
Part of a team that plans and creates games for mobile devices
Assist in generating reports based on user feedback on interactive gaming elements
Provide management with summary reports of ideas and concepts generated during team meetings
Answer technical questions about games in development during meetings with clients

School Years 2010–2013: **Website Programmer**, Massachusetts Institute of Technology, Electrical Engineering and Computer Science Department
Assisted in redesigning the department website
Gathered and updated data
Assisted in fixing cross-compatibility issues
Tested and debugged page functions

Summer 2012: **Mobile Application Developer Intern, Baldar Technologies**
Participated in full app development cycle
Created technical specifications for mobile apps
Tested mobile apps and recorded results

Summer 2011: **Computer Lab Assistant, Bridgeport Public Library**
Assisted computer lab users with software issues
Diagnosed and fixed network problems
Updated software and maintained usage records

## SKILLS AND TOOLS
• Technically certified in multiple mobile operating software platforms
• Strong communication and presentation skills
• Experience working under tight deadlines
• Highly developed eye for detail
• Excellent creative problem-solving abilities
• Knowledgeable in database management and security protocols

HTML5; C++; Java; Ruby on Rails; Python; Swift; Microsoft Office Suite; Adobe Creative Suite

References available upon request.

*This is an example of a résumé for a mobile app developer. A successful résumé clearly details the applicant's experience and skills.*

find out about openings from friends, teachers, and former coworkers. Online forums can also be a good place to find out about jobs from people working in the field.

Some internships can turn into full-time positions if you've made a good impression. The same is true with summer jobs. Those experiences help you make connections with other professionals and can lead to future opportunities.

Building your network before you graduate can give you a good start on finding a job. Become friendly with faculty members and alumni. Many alumni who need to fill job openings turn to their colleges for recruits who have the right skills. Similarly, professors may be in touch with former students who need to hire people for app development work.

Many high schools and colleges participate in career fairs. At these events, recruiters from different companies—both larger and well-established firms and smaller start-ups—gather to share information and meet potential applicants. Some career fairs are general and feature employers from multiple industries. Others are targeted toward the tech industry. Recruiters at these events often take résumés, answer questions, and hand out information about their companies.

Recruiters may come to your campus for recruitment drives. These efforts usually consist of a single company that sets up a table or booth where students learn about job opportunities. Like career fairs, you'll likely be able to hand off a résumé and ask questions. Find out what the recruiter's company is looking for and take that information into consideration if you decide to apply. You can address those points in your cover letter. Even if you're still far from graduation, these events can be a great way to learn what companies want from their new hires.

The continuing popularity of mobile devices such as smartphones and tablets means that mobile app developers will be in demand for some years to come. Because mobile

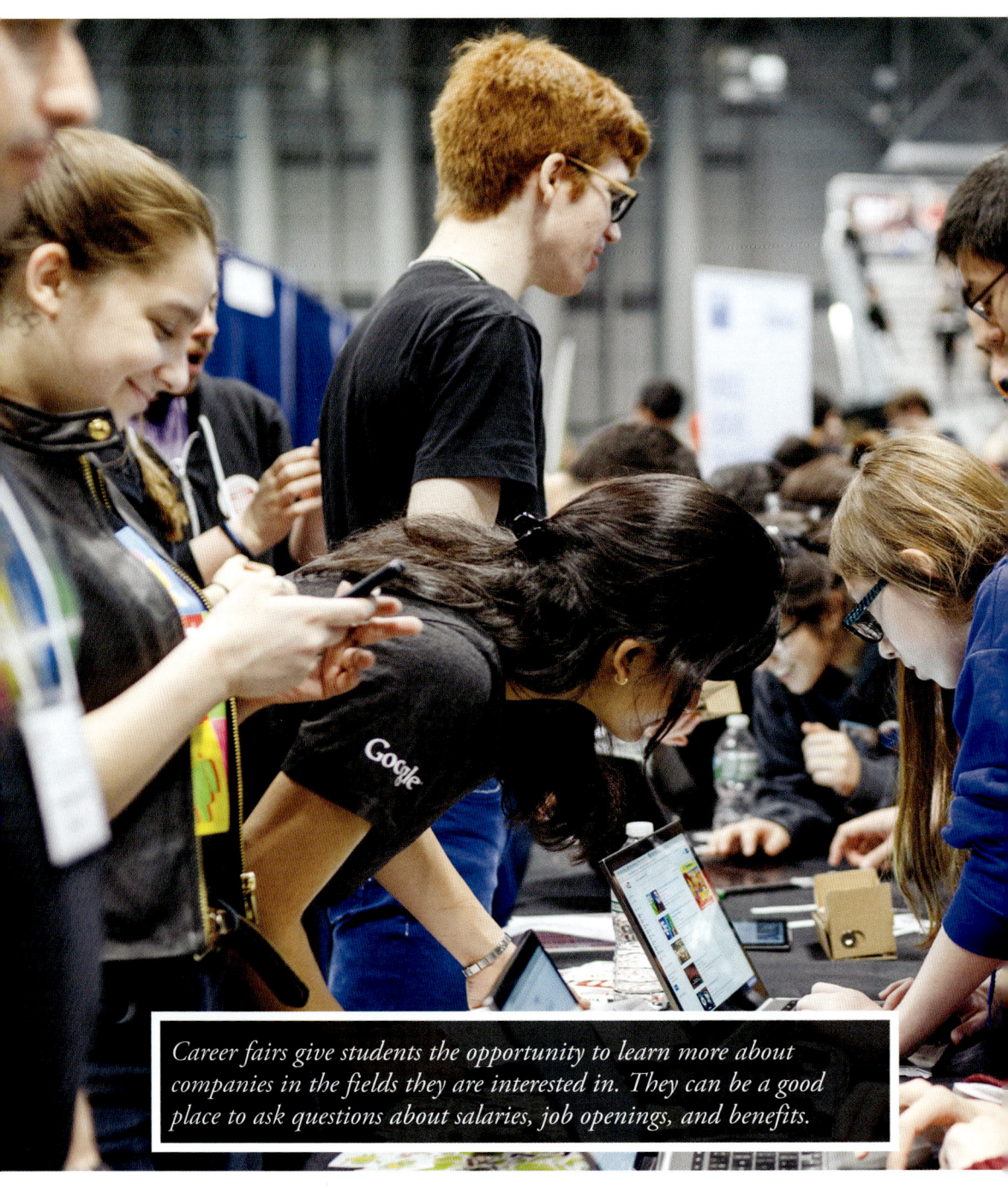

Career fairs give students the opportunity to learn more about companies in the fields they are interested in. They can be a good place to ask questions about salaries, job openings, and benefits.

apps can cover so many different fields, these positions are actually open in a variety of industries.

The *Occupational Outlook Handbook*, a publication produced and updated by the Bureau of Labor Statistics (BLS), indicates that the software development career field is expected to grow by about 17 percent through 2024, increasing from 1,114,000 positions in 2014 to an estimated 1,300,600 in 2024. Applications developers are part of that trend, with approximately 747,730 such positions reported by the BLS in 2015 and annual growth at 1.4 percent.

# chapter 5

# APP DEVELOPMENT OPPORTUNITIES

Mobile app developers work in diverse types of places. If you are hired by a large firm such as Apple, you may find yourself working in big computer labs situated within enormous campuses. Small start-ups often have cozy office setups and may even feel cramped, though the smaller spaces can lead to stronger collaboration between workers. If you are working freelance, you can do your mobile app development work in the comfort of your own home, communicating with coworkers through chat, phone calls, and email.

## ON THE JOB

Mobile app developers often work within team environments. Several developers will work on various aspects of one app, with the pieces fitting together to make the finished product. Collaborative atmospheres are encouraged so that everyone feels comfortable sharing ideas with other people on the team, as well as pointing out potential problems.

The workload for mobile app developers can be intense. They work under tight deadlines and often have to meet multiple goals before the project is complete. They have to make sure that every element of the app they've created is working perfectly before it is released to the public. When projects are completed, teams may brainstorm to come up with new mobile apps or to find ways to upgrade old apps. Everyone contributes, adding their own ideas and suggesting tweaks. The team sets goals and parameters for these mobile apps, deciding exactly what they will do and setting development schedules.

The job can be hard at the beginning. Even if you had excellent grades in all your computer science classes, you probably won't be able to do everything perfectly at first. Your apps may be rejected several times before you get everything right. You will have to be persistent until you find what's wrong, whether it's a usability issue or an error in the code. Mobile app developers often seek feedback from other developers on ways to make an app better or even for help in spotting errors. Your team members will likely be ready to help you.

*Mobile app developers often work in collaborative environments in which every member of the team can feel free to contribute their ideas.*

*Testing is a vital step in developing mobile apps. Fixing flaws can be a lengthy process that sometimes requires hours of scanning code to spot the problem.*

Even as you gain experience, you will be challenged to keep up with changes to the platforms. Mobile platforms evolve constantly, and app developers have to be aware of those changes. Working with other mobile app developers as part of a team will help you stay ahead of those changes.

Once the mobile app is completed, it is tested over and over. Bigger companies may have quality assurance professionals who do nothing but test software for flaws. In smaller firms and start-ups, all of the testing might be done by the development team. Testing consists of using and even misusing the app in every way imaginable to see if everything works as it should. Any flaws that are spotted are corrected before the final product is released.

## AREAS OF GROWTH

There are numerous ways in which people use their mobile apps, and there are millions of apps available for users to

Mobile apps such as Snapchat allow users to edit their photos with a wide range of tools and easily share them with friends.

download. There are several types of apps that are generally in high demand. Entertainment apps are consistently popular. Developers are constantly finding ways to innovate in the field and create new mobile apps that offer users what they want. These mobile apps include games, as well as video and music players. YouTube, Pandora Radio, and Netflix all fall within this category.

Mobile social media applications such as Facebook, Snapchat, and Pinterest enable people to share their photos and videos from their mobile devices. A large number of mobile apps also enable users to take better photos and videos, as well as providing editing tools. These include Enlight and Instagram.

Service applications are heavily used, and there are always possibilities for creating new mobile apps that put a new spin on ideas such as mapping, car sharing, reviews, and shopping. Many stores

## WEARABLE TECHNOLOGY APPS

Smartphones are extremely portable, but efforts have been underway for several years to create wireless internet technology in even smaller packages. Companies such as Apple and Google are working to embed mobile tech in products such as Google Glass eyewear and smartwatches such as the Apple Watch, which are already available. Mobile apps that can track data such as the wearer's cholesterol levels can be found for the Apple Watch. Google Glass mobile apps can be used to access and view a wide variety of data, capture images, and stream video through voice commands. Developers are even working on building tiny computers that can attach to a person's skin, opening up numerous new possibilities for creative mobile app developers.

and businesses are even beginning to offer electronic payment options, in which customers use smartphones to make payments. These apps have to interact with scanners while also accessing your preferred payment method, making security a priority for the mobile app developers who build them.

The development of affordable home automation technology gives users the ability to control systems throughout their homes through their smartphones by using mobile apps; mobile apps interact with technology inside specially designed thermostats, lights, appliances, and other objects to allow the user to operate them from afar.

## JOB SECURITY

Mobile app developers are highly sought after by a wide variety of employers, from large software companies to small start-ups, as well as businesses such as department stores, restaurant chains, banks, and health care companies. Once the mobile app development cycle becomes second nature to them, they may begin taking on more responsibility for the team. They may come to lead the team or even branch out to begin a start-up business.

There's less job stability for freelance mobile app developers, but developing a good reputation can lead to enough repeat business and referrals to keep you busy. Knowing how to create mobile apps across multiple platforms can help freelancers take on a wide range of jobs from many interesting employers. A willingness to learn new development platforms and coding languages can help build that client base, ensuring steady work.

## WHERE TO WORK

The IT industry is constantly growing, but there are a few places where most of the jobs are concentrated. If there are no openings in your region, you may want to look for jobs in places where the IT industry has a strong presence. Many big cities have major tech hubs where mobile app developers might find work. These include places such as Seattle, Washington; San Francisco, California; Chicago, Illinois; and Austin, Texas. Some larger college towns also have technology companies nearby, particularly if the local college has a strong computer science department.

Freelance mobile app developers may be able to work remotely, meaning they don't have to appear at an office every day. They can do their work anywhere, even hundreds or thousands of miles away. Other freelancers may have to report to their employers on a weekly or monthly basis, requiring them to travel.

Where you'll live isn't the only factor to consider when it comes to deciding whether or not to accept a job offer. You

*Freelancing gives mobile app developers the chance to set their own schedules and work from the comfort of their own homes.*

should also look at the company's culture. Find out how employees are treated beyond details such as salary and benefits. Is their work valued? Are there problems with how the company operates? Seek out current or former employees who might be able to give you details about the company. There are also websites that publish reviews of workplaces. They can help you gain an idea of how the company is run and how employees are treated. Ideally, your mobile app development position will give you ample opportunities to learn and grow with the company, while allowing you to maintain a healthy balance between your home life and work.

# glossary

**application**  App for short; a piece of computer software designed to do a particular job. Mobile apps are software programs that run on smartphones, tablets, or other portable devices.

**bandwidth**  The amount of data that can be transmitted over a computer network or internet connection in a specific amount of time.

**browser**  A computer program that allows users to search for information and view websites on the internet.

**certification**  Proof that a person possesses certain skills or qualities.

**code**  A set of instructions for a computer to follow.

**collaborative**  Involving a group of people working together to meet a certain goal.

**compatible**  Able to exist and perform together in harmony.

**computer science**  The branch of engineering that deals with computer hardware and software.

**data**  Information that can be transmitted or processed by digital means.

**database**  A structured collection of data that is stored on a computer.

**developer**  A person who designs and builds software applications.

**freelancer**  Someone who works in a profession without being committed to a single employer.

**intern**  A student in a specialized field who is gaining professional experience under supervision.

**network**  To remain in contact with certain people and groups, particularly for the purpose of sharing professional information.

**platform** The computer equipment that uses a particular form of operating system.

**portfolio** A collection of samples showing a person's best professional work.

**program** A series of instructions that makes a computer perform a certain task or action.

**smartphone** A mobile phone that also works as a small computer, allowing users to run programs and store data.

**software** Programs that are used by computers for doing certain jobs.

**start-up** A newly launched company or business.

**tablet** A mobile computing device that is flat and rectangular, controlled by a touchscreen, and usually used for reading, accessing the internet, and other activities.

**transaction** The act of buying or selling something or making a business deal.

# for more information

Bureau of Labor Statistics (BLS)
Postal Square Building
2 Massachusetts Avenue NE
Washington, DC 20212
(202) 691-5200
Website: http://www.bls.gov
Facebook: @departmentoflabor
Twitter: @BLS_gov
The Bureau of Labor Statistics is an agency within the US
    Department of Labor dedicated to gathering data about
    the labor market, working conditions, and the career
    outlook for many jobs. Each year, the BLS updates the
    *Occupational Outlook Handbook* (http://www.bls.gov
    /ooh), which provides information about thousands of
    careers, job requirements, and average salaries.

Canada's Association of IT Professionals (CIPS)
National Office
5090 Explorer Drive, Suite 801
Mississauga, ON L4W 4T9
Canada
(905) 602-1370
Website: http://www.cips.ca
Facebook: @CIPS-Canadas-Association-of-IT-Professionals
Twitter: @CIPS
CIPS is an organization dedicated to setting standards and
    establishing best practices for Canada's information tech-
    nology professionals.

Computer History Museum
1401 North Shoreline Boulevard
Mountain View, CA 94043
(650) 810-1010
Website: http://www.computerhistory.org
Facebook: @computerhistory
Twitter: @computerhistory
The mission of the Computer History Museum is to preserve
    and present for posterity the artifacts and stories of the
    information age.

Entertainment Software Association (ESA)
601 Massachusetts Avenue NW, Suite 300
Washington, DC 20001
Website: http://www.theesa.com
Facebook: @TheEntertainmentSoftwareAssociation
Twitter: @RichatESA
The ESA provides professional and support services to com-
    panies that create computer and video games for consoles,
    computers, mobile devices, and the internet.

Internet Society
1775 Wiehle Avenue, Suite 201
Reston, VA 20190-5108
(703) 439-2120
Website: http://www.isoc.org
Facebook: @InternetSociety
Twitter: @internetsociety
This organization works to address issues relating to the inter-
    net, including internet education, standards, and policy.

Media Awareness Network
1500 Merivale Road, Third Floor
Ottawa, ON K2E 6Z5

Canada
(613) 224-7721
Website: http://www.media-awareness.ca/english/index.cfm
The website for Media Awareness Network contains a selection of digital literacy resources for students, teachers, and parents.

National Science Foundation (NSF)
4201 Wilson Boulevard
Arlington, VA 22230
(703) 292-5111
Website: http://www.nsf.gov
Facebook: @US.NSF
Twitter: @NSF
The NSF is a government agency that funds scientific research in a variety of fields, including computer and information science and engineering and cyberinfrastructure training.

## WEBSITES

Because of the changing nature of internet links, Rosen Publishing has developed an online list of websites related to the subject of this book. This site is updated regularly. Please use this link to access the list:

http://www.rosenlinks.com/ECAR/App

# for further reading

Bedell, Jane. *So, You Want to Be a Coder?: The Ultimate Guide to a Career in Programming, Video Game Creation, Robotics, and More!* (Be What You Want). New York, NY: Aladdin/Beyond Words, 2016.

Foege, Alec. *The Tinkerers: The Amateurs, DIYers, and Inventors Who Make America Great.* New York, NY: Basic Books, 2013.

Furgang, Kathy. *Money-Making Opportunities for Teens Who Are Computer Savvy* (Make Money Now!). New York, NY: Rosen Publishing, 2014.

Harmon, Daniel. *Powering Up a Career in Software Development and Programming* (Preparing for Tomorrow's Careers). New York, NY: Rosen Publishing, 2016.

Marji, Majed. *Learn to Program with Scratch: A Visual Introduction to Programming with Art, Science, Math and Games.* San Francisco, CA: No Starch Press, 2014.

Matthes, Eric. *Python Crash Course: A Hands-On, Project-Based Introduction to Programming.* San Francisco, CA: No Starch Press, 2015.

Nagle, Jeanne. *Getting to Know Scratch* (Code Power: A Teen Programmer's Guide). New York, NY: Rosen Publishing, 2015.

Niver, Heather Moore. *Careers for Tech Girls in Computer Science* (Tech Girls). New York, NY: Rosen Publishing, 2016.

Payment, Simone. *Getting to Know Python* (Code Power: A Teen Programmer's Guide). New York, NY: Rosen Publishing, 2015.

Stanley, Erin. *Career Building Through Creating Mobile Apps* (Digital Career Building). New York, NY: Rosen Publishing, 2014.

# bibliography

Glasser, J. D. *Secure Development for Mobile Apps: How to Design and Code Secure Mobile Applications with PHP and JavaScript.* Boca Raton, FL: CRC Press, 2015.

Golson, Jordan. "Apple's App Store Now Has Over 2 Million Apps." The Verge, June 13, 2016. http://www.theverge.com /2016/6/13/11922926/apple-apps-2-million-wwdc-2016.

Kanellos, Michael. "Moore's Law to Roll on for Another Decade." CNET, February 11, 2003. https://www.cnet .com/news/moores-law-to-roll-on-for-another-decade.

Mehrotra, Anushka. "Move Over College Students. Silicon Valley Turns to High Schools for Interns." *USA Today College*, July 22, 2014. http://college.usatoday.com /2014/07/22/move-over-college-students-silicon-valley -turns-to-high-schools-for-interns.

Pagliery, Jose. "Nearly One Million Android Phones Infected by Hackers." CNN, November 30, 2016. http://money .cnn.com/2016/11/30/technology/android-phones-infected.

PayScale. "Mobile Applications Developer Salary (United States)." Retrieved March 14, 2017. http://www.payscale .com/research/US/Job=Mobile_Applications_Developer /Salary.

Perez, Sarah. "Consumers Spend 85% of Time on Smartphones in Apps, but Only 5 Apps See Heavy Use. "TechCrunch, June 22, 2015. https://techcrunch.com/2015/06/22 /consumers-spend-85-of-time-on-smartphones-in-apps -but-only-5-apps-see-heavy-use.

Pew Research Center. "Mobile Fact Sheet." January 12, 2017. http://www.pewinternet.org/fact-sheet/mobile.

Protalinski, Emil. "Hey Microsoft, How Many Apps Are in the Windows Store?" VentureBeat, March 30, 2016.

http://venturebeat.com/2016/03/30/hey-microsoft-how
-many-apps-are-in-the-windows-store.

Rajput, Mehul. "Tracing the History and Evolution of Mobile
Apps." TECH.CO, November 27, 2015. http://tech.co
/mobile-app-history-evolution-2015-11.

Rossi, Ben. "Current and Future Applications for Wearable
Technology." Information Age, December 8, 2015. http://
www.information-age.com/current-and-future
-applications-wearable-technology-123460636.

Rossignol, Joe. "What You Need to Know About iOS Malware
XcodeGhost." MacRumors, September 20, 2015. https://
www.macrumors.com/2015/09/20/xcodeghost
-chinese-malware-faq.

Stackpole, Beth. "Your Next Job: Mobile App Developer?"
Computerworld, June 27, 2011. http://www
.computerworld.com/article/2509463/app-development
/your-next-job--mobile-app-developer-.html.

Strain, Matt. "1983 to Today: A History of Mobile Apps."
Guardian, February 13, 2015. https://www
.theguardian.com/media-network/2015/feb/13/history
-mobile-apps-future-interactive-timeline.

Taylor, Allan, and James Robert Parish. Career Opportunities in
the Internet, Video Games, and Multimedia. New York, NY:
Checkmark Books, 2007.

US Department of Labor, Bureau of Labor Statistics.
Occupational Outlook Handbook. December 17, 2015.
https://www.bls.gov/ooh/home.htm.

Viswanathan, Priya. "How to Write an Impressive Mobile App
Developer Resume." Lifewire, October 19, 2016. https://
www.lifewire.com/how-to-write-an-impressive
-mobile-app-developer-resume-2373170.

White, Carla. Idea to iPhone: The Essential Guide to Creating Your
First App for the iPhone and iPad. Hoboken, NJ: Wiley, 2013.

Yate, Martin. Knock 'em Dead: The Ultimate Job Search Guide
2017. Avon, MA: Adams Media, 2016.

# index

## ABOUT THE AUTHOR

Jason Porterfield is a writer and journalist living in Chicago, Illinois, where he writes about tech subjects for several publications. Some of his technology books include *Julian Assange and WikiLeaks*; *Tim Berners-Lee, Niklas Zennström and Skype*; *Angry Birds and Rovio Entertainment*; *White and Black Hat Hackers*; *Careers as a Cyberterrorism Expert*; and *Conducting Basic and Advanced Searches*.

## PHOTO CREDITS

Cover, p. 1 (figure) Aaron Amat/Shutterstock.com; cover, p. 1 (background) Billion Photos/Shutterstock.com; pp. 4–5 Denys Prykhodov/Shutterstock.com; p. 8 dennizn/Shutterstock.com; pp. 10–11, 44–45, 64 © AP Images; p. 14 Bloomberg/Getty Images; pp. 16–17 Syda Productions/Shutterstock.com; pp. 22–23 Vintage Tone/Shutterstock.com; pp. 24–25 ymgerman/Shutterstock.com; pp. 26–27 Sander Koning/AFP /Getty Images; pp. 30–31 omgimages/iStock/Thinkstock; pp. 34–35 Hero Images/Getty Images; pp. 38–39 Akron Beacon Journal/Tribune News Service/Getty Images; pp. 40–41 Thomas Barwick/Taxi/Getty Images; pp. 50–51 Christian Science Monitor/Getty Images; pp. 54–55 sturti/E+/Getty Images; pp. 58–59 Richard Levine/Corbis News/Getty Images; pp. 61, 62–63 dotshock/Shutterstock.com; p. 67 JGalione/E+ /Getty Images.

Design: Matt Cauli; Layout: Tahara Anderson; Senior Editor: Kathy Kuhtz Campbell; Photo Research: Karen Huang